CREATURE LOVING VOLUME 3
Lilith Leana

Table of Contents

Acknowledgement

A big thank you to my husband for always believing in me and never making me feel like I couldn't do it.

Cover art

Cover art from Depositphoto

Cover design

Lilith Leana with Canva

Brief Summary

Bedding the God of Dreams

Roya has always been able to control her dreams, until one evening. She meets the God of Dreams and decides that he can show her the real pleasures that dreams have to offer.

The God of Dreams lives a lonely life, visiting people's dreams but never participating. That is, until he meets Roya. She appears in his court, ready to live out all her dreams.

Saved by the Grim Reaper

Lila has been surrounded by death on her birthday all her life. On her 33rd birthday, she decides to be alone, but an earthquake traps her inside her cabin, taking her last breath.

The Grim Reaper has been following Lila all her life, and when she is about the die, he saves her. When she wakes up, Lila isn't appealed by his monstrous face, she asks him to save her in more ways than one.

Chased by the Werewolf

Shay goes to her first monthly Monster - Human mixer to get her mind off her ex. She didn't expect to meet a handsome werewolf who wants to chase her. She agrees and readies herself for the running of a lifetime.

Mason smells a delicious new human at the monthly mixer and immediately knows he needs to make her his. He doesn't want to scare her but his primal urges threaten to take over. When she runs, no one can hold him back to claim her as his.

Trapped with the Yeti

Alice goes to visit her best friend and Yeti family. She is attracted to her grumpy Yeti guide, and when they get trapped together during a storm, she acts on her desires.

Seth, the Yeti doesn't like humans since he thinks they are all weak and tiny. When Alice proves she can take him, his urge to breed her awakens. He will never let this small human go.

A Mate for the Vampire Queen

The Vampire Queen was busy with a war looming close by and didn't have time for the outrageous claims of a Beta Wolf Shifter. But when she tasted his blood she had to admit that her attraction to him went deeper than she had ever imagined.

Beta Isaac goes to the Vampire Queen to forge an alliance with his Pack. He never imagined finding his Mate in the ancient, cold woman, but he will never let her go.

Going to a Naga Wedding

After dating for a year Avery joins Ezra at his cousin's weddings. She didn't expect it to be so... overly familial.

Ezra is excited for Avery to meet his family but he hadn't realized that Naga customs are very different from the other weddings Avery has been to.

READER ADVISORY: THIS story contains explicit sex scenes.

Creature Loving Volume 3 is a collection of five previously published standalone short erotic stories and one exciting new bonus story.

It is filled with human FMC's loving Monsters, Beasts and Creatures. Explicit sex scenes, standalone, no cheating or cliffhangers.

Bedding the God of Dreams

I have always been able to control my dreams. Until this one. As soon as I went to sleep, I knew something was off.

Usually, I could control my entire dream from start to finish. I tended to come up with a general script of what I wanted to happen, and it played out with some variations, but it still followed my script. Like any other person, I also had nightmares, but as soon as I was aware of them, I could control them or I could wake up.

I will be honest, 95 percent of my dreams were sex dreams. A girl has needs, and since I was single, I got my sexual fulfillment through my dreams, with the characters I created. I could imagine any kind of scenario, with any kind and any number of creatures. So why would I ever need to date?

This dream started out the same way. I had just finished a delectable reverse harem monster book, so obviously, that inspired my dream. I was being double stuffed and pleasured by all kinds of monsters when something strange happened.

It felt like the electricity went out in my brain. My entire dream just disappeared, and I was left alone in the dark. A chill went through me, and I pulled my arms around my naked body. I imagined clothing to appear, but it didn't come like it normally did.

Suddenly, a deep, ethereal voice sounded through the darkness.

"Who are you?"

"Roya," I whispered, not daring to speak too loud for fear of angering the bodiless voice. Nothing like this had ever happened before, so I knew to proceed with caution.

"What are you doing here, Roya?"

The deep rumble of the voice send shivers through my body and I clasped my arms more firmly around me. I really wished I had some clothing right now. Never before had I felt lost in a dream, and I didn't like the feeling.

"I don't know. I just want to get back or wake up."

"So you know this is a dream?"

I was getting annoyed. This faceless voice wasn't offering me any advice, and I just wanted out.

"Of course I do. Show yourself or let me get back to what I was doing."

A bright light appeared before me, and I had to squint to be able to see it. A dark, winged figure floated towards me. The closer he got, the better I could make out his tall, dark form, framed by two massive black wings. It was hard to describe him. He seemed to glow light and dark at the same time. His face was pale, his hair dark, and his eyes looked like the night sky, twinkling in the light.

"Who are you?" I asked, breathless, enamored by his appearance.

He smiled thinly.

"I have many names, Oneiro, Morpheus, Phantasus, Somnia, Phobetor, the Sandman. But you can call me the God of Dreams."

I laughed out loud, the sounds of my amusement filling up the empty air around me. I had made up a lot of stuff in my head, but this certainly took the cake.

"I'm not gonna call you 'God of Dreams,'" I said, using air quotes around his name. "That's a mouth full. I'll call you Ony."

In a flash, he was only a hair away from my face. His hauntingly beautiful face contorted in anger. His starry eyes darkened like a storm and the smile fell off my face.

"You dare defy a King in his own court? A God in his own world? A Creator in his own realm?"

His booming voice sent shivers through my body. This was more than a mere dream, I realized it too late. What I knew for certain about dreams was that you should never show your fear. I took a deep breath to calm my fluttering heart.

"I do," I said, bracing for his wrath.

A low, throaty chuckle resounded. It sounded rusty like he hadn't used it in a long time. His stormy eyes lightened and I could see more stars twinkle in them.

"It has been a while since someone defied me," he said with a small quirk in his mouth.

I smiled back. "It has been a while since a dream got away from me." I bit my lip and leaned a bit closer. "Usually I call the shots in my dream."

"Do you now?" the God of Dreams said, not moving away. "I have seen all the dreams in my realm, but I don't think I have seen yours."

"I can show you if you want?"

"Would you be so kind?"

"More selfish than kind," I replied, focusing my eyes on his lips.

I hadn't gotten the usual release that I got from my dreams yet. His lips drew me in. Dreaming of desire and arousal was definitely not the same as experiencing it for real. I didn't know where I was, but it was somewhere between a dream and real life. It felt more real than any dream I had experienced so far, and I wanted to experience more of it with him.

His eyes shot to my lips as well. A low sound of need filled the empty space between us. I didn't know which one of us made it, but it didn't matter. All that mattered was this moment; this attraction that lingered between us.

"It has been ages since I let myself indulge in the pleasures of the flesh," he said.

"Indulge in me, oh God of Dreams," I whispered.

Adding his title had the desired effect. He closed the gap between us, and his lips met mine. The kiss was everything I had ever dreamed of, and somehow at the same time, so much more. I moaned in his mouth, reveling in the all-encompassing taste of his lips. He tasted like all of my dreams, a swirl of my hopes and desires mixed into a delicious cocktail unique to my taste. Impossible to describe, but the most delicious sensation ever.

His arms wrapped around me, making me feel safe and cherished by him. A weird thought about someone I just met, but it felt right somehow. He felt familiar. People spend about a third of their lives asleep, not knowing what happened to them. I remembered all my dreams since I created them. Somehow, I didn't think I created him. This felt like something far more real than a dream.

The God of Dreams pulled me close to him. His hard body met my soft one, and I moaned from the arousing sensation. His tongue slipped between my lips meeting mine. It was slick, soft, and delicious. He discovered my mouth as I let him take over. I loved not having to orchestrate everything. I could just enjoy the experience and react naturally to what he was doing to me.

Suddenly, I could feel the world tilt on its ax. I wasn't standing anymore. I was lying on a soft bed of something... It didn't have a shape or form that I recognized or could describe. Blackness surrounded us, and all I could see was him. It was like he was emitting light from himself. I could see him as clearly as day, but right behind him, there was only a vast space of nothing.

I focused on him again, gazing into those beautiful, starry eyes. He kissed his way down my body, lingering in every pleasurable location. His soft lips awakened something deep inside of me. My body responded, my nipples tightened, goosebumps spread over my skin, and I could feel wetness seep out between my legs.

He took his time at my breasts, licking and nipping at my hardened nipples. Shivers of delight went through me, and I could feel pleasure building up inside of me. Once he was satisfied with my pleasured breasts, he moved lower, kissing every inch he encountered. His soft lips and wet tongue traced a delicious path down my body.

Arriving between my legs, he moved closer to my pussy. Taking a deep breath, he took in my scent and moaned sexually. A shiver racked my body, and my pussy clenched around nothing, emitting more wetness.

"I wonder if you taste as good as you smell," he whispered, leaning closer.

His hot breath heated my pussy. I was ready to beg for more when he moved closer and swiped his tongue between my pussy lips. Sparks of pleasure burst as I gasped, and a low, guttural moan came from him. The sound was so utterly delicious and sexual that I moaned in response. He dove back down, licking me in full earnest.

"You. Taste. Like. A. Dream."

Each word was accentuated by a flick of his tongue. Slowly, the pleasure started to rise. His tongue worked between my pussy lips. The sounds that left him only added to my arousal. The feeling inside of me grew, and his delicious mouth added more pleasure. My body started to tremble, close to my climax. With only his mouth and talented tongue, he could take me to heights that most of the figments of my imagination had to use entire arsenals of toys for.

He felt so good, so right, so mine? The words came into my mind without me wanting them. The God of Dreams couldn't be mine. He belonged to no one, but he also belonged to us all.

What would our world look like without dreams?

My thoughts disappeared when he focused on my clit with his delicious mouth. His tongue circled around my pleasure bud, and he entered one long finger into my tight pussy. It felt too good to describe, too good to bear. It was everything at once and nothing I had ever experienced before.

When he sucked on clit, my climax burst, and I exploded with a pleasurable cry. Little sparks flew through the surrounding darkness. Eyes wide, mouth open, I gazed upon the stars forming around us. It resembled his eyes, but with every color in existence. It was beautiful and ethereal, nothing like I could have ever come up with myself.

My body trembled with the last shivers of pleasure that coursed through me. My mind tried to catch up, but I was too filled with pleasure that it had a hard time working properly.

He floated on top of me, his powerful wings holding him up in the air. The stars we had created together surrounded him. His hungry, twinkling eyes racked across my body.

"I need to have you now," he growled out.

His voice was low and full of need. I nodded, not trusting my own voice. In a blink of an eye, he was as naked as I was. I tried to remember what he had been wearing, but there was a blankness in my mind.

I looked at his body, seeing it clearly for the first time. His skin was the color of the night sky, and his form was hard to describe. It seemed almost to change as soon as my mind made up what he looked like. The only thing that stayed the same was his beautiful eyes. His eyes were the window to his soul, showing me every single emotion going through him. Each flicker, and twinkle of the stars in them I could recognize as a thought or an emotion.

I focused on his eyes. They lit up with passion; the stars swirling in them, trying to suck me in. I could only feel, and not think anymore, only feel him, us together.

A presence at my entrance startled me. When I looked down, I could see his cock pushing at my pussy, requesting access. His cock looked like a tornado, sucking my attention to it. Magnificent, massive, and ready to fill me. I opened my legs wide to accommodate him, and with one thrust, he sunk inside of me. He fitted perfectly, not too small, not too big, just the right size for me to feel the absolute height of pleasure.

"You feel amazing," I moaned out, squeezing my muscles around him, willing him to move.

"You do too, Roya," he replied.

He started to move, with his eyes locked on mine. Every movement touched me just right. Every thrust sparked pleasure points inside of me. Every sound he made only enhanced my arousal. The pleasure inside of me grew. More and more coursed through my body, taking me higher and higher.

Suddenly, his arms wrapped around me, and we soared up into the air. I could feel my skin being caressed by the wind. Every flap of his wings corresponded to a thrust of his cock. The higher we flew, the bigger the pleasure inside of me became. I could feel his cock thrust and pull, and I could feel his wings work to get us higher. It felt heavenly, otherworldly, amazing. So many words to describe it, and none of them felt adequate.

I felt ready to come, but I needed just something more. As if he could read my thoughts, a flick over my clit made me look down. There was nothing there. I could see his cock pummeling into me, and the sight made me moan with pleasure. He fit perfectly, stretching my pussy just right so I felt stuffed to the brink. Then again, I could feel a flick over my clit which made me arch with pleasure.

"I will pleasure you with my body, and my mind, my sweet Roya," he said.

His booming voice filled my head, and I could feel it vibrate through my body. I didn't know how, but somehow he was pleasuring me with his mind, and it was absolutely perfect. Each thrust with his cock pushed every pleasure point inside of me in sync with the flicks of his mind over my clit. Tremors coursed through my body, and his next thrust was enough to set me off. Waves of pleasure washed over me, moans and gasps escaping my mouth as my pussy clenched around his cock.

"Hold on," he whispered in my ear, while my body shook with pleasure.

Before my brain could process his words, at the height of my climax, he dove down. I felt weightless for a moment. That falling sensation you sometimes get in dreams, very present. My body seized up, and adrenaline rushed through me, only enhancing my orgasm. The waves of pleasure washed over me, feeling more intense than ever. My brain prepared for an impact, while my body could only feel the pleasure. I braced for a crash that never came.

Suddenly, the softest of clouds surrounded me. My body was floating between them, and I reveled in the comfortable, fluffy feeling. He was still inside of me. With my body perched up against the delicate clouds, he thrust into me again. He could leverage me better, thrust into me harder, and let me fly higher with pleasure. His eyes became feverish with passion. I could see that he was holding himself back. I wanted all of him.

"More," I moaned. "Give me all of it."

I could feel another climax grow and threaten to break me. Words and sounds of pleasure and desire left me without a conscious thought of myself. His eyes grew hotter and I could almost feel the electricity in the air.

After another thrust that hit just the right spot inside of me, it flooded my scenes. Tremors of pleasure racked my body, until I felt weightless, floating around through the sky, through the clouds, still wrapped in his arms.

The God of Dreams took on a leisurely pace now. Filling me slow and gently. Pulling out, and pushing into me again, and again. A spark inside of me grew again, and I could feel my body preparing for another orgasm. This time I needed him to come with me, to join me in the world of pleasure and release he had shown me.

"Please," I whispered, my voice hoarse with all the pleasurable screams I have uttered. "Come with me. Feel the pleasure I feel. Enjoy our time together."

He listened to my words. His eyes were so full of emotions that it seemed as if the light would burst from them. His thrusts gained momentum, his whole body taut with the release that was so close.

"I will, my dear Roya," he said in a low, husky voice.

I could feel his cock throbbing inside of me, expanding, thrusting, and then suddenly filling me with his cum. The feeling of being stuffed and filled by him triggered my next orgasm. Waves of pleasure washed over me, gentle this time. Instead of breaking me and showing me all the things I had never experienced before, they soothed me. The pleasure filling me took me high and gently let me down on top of it.

I felt boneless, and weightless, pleasured as I had never been before. His eyes softened, the lights in them dimming to a soft glow, still so hauntingly beautiful. He leaned over and gave me a soft kiss on my forehead.

"Wake well, my dear Roya. Until next time," he said in that deep, soft soothing voice, and I could feel myself slipping away from the dream back into the land of the wake.

When would I see him again? Would it be in another dream?

The End

Saved by the Grim Reaper

I have always been surrounded by death on my birthday. The day I was born my mother didn't survive. The year after my dad passed away. Every single year without a fault someone I cared about died. So I decided to not let people close to me anymore. I had no family left, and I had cut off my surviving friends right after my last birthday when I lost my best friend. It was for their own good.

So I was celebrating my 33 birthday all alone in some cabin in the woods. Maybe this year it would be my turn and I could break the curse.

I put out all the remembrance cards of the people that I lost. I hated that my collection kept growing, but this year would be the last.

I had done some research, focusing on what could be the reason for my misfortune. It didn't help that I was born on the 2nd of November, the day of the dead. But that alone couldn't be it. There were millions of people that shared my birthday and didn't have the same back luck following them around. I even met some of them, just to be sure.

Looking at each card, I said my goodbye to them as I did every year. I started with my mothers. Her card was almost ready for the landfill, but I couldn't get rid of it. It was the only picture I had of her. I touched it with gentle fingers, running across her face that was so similar to mine. She looked so young, and full of life smiling into the camera. I laid it next to that of my father. They looked like such a happy couple. I wish I had known them.

When I bend down to pick up the next card, a rumble shook the earth. I froze, not knowing what to do. An earthquake racked the ground, and before I could react a massive crack resounded. Just when I looked up, the ceiling started coming down and everything went dark.

I was going to die. On my birthday. At least that meant the end of my curse. Not the way I had wanted, but there would be no other victims on my birthday at last.

I was trapped beneath the rubble of the ceiling of the small cabin. My phone was too far, and I was all alone in the woods. No one knew where I was, so no one would come searching for me. They might find me next year when the owners of the cabin would come back.

A lone tear escaped me, gliding across my cheek, clearing away the dust that had settled there. "Happy last birthday to me," I whispered in the dark.

"Not on my watch," a deep rumbling voice said.

I tried to look at where the sound had come from, but I couldn't move. The comfort of knowing that I wasn't alone in my last moments, made me smile. I closed my eyes and let the darkness take over.

The next sensation was warmth. I didn't know how much time had passed, but I wasn't underneath the rubble anymore. I was in a soft bed, surrounded by strong arms. I wanted to look behind me, but I couldn't move.

"Sleep Lila. You're safe now. Just sleep and heal," that same deep rumbling voice whispered in my ear.

Somehow I knew I could trust him, so I listened and slept again.

It felt like I was constantly between sleeping, dying, and living. I had no idea how much time passed while I was in that floating-place between realms, but I knew that my body was healing, and someone was taking care of me.

When I woke up again, I could feel that my body was whole and healthy. I opened my eyes and I could see a figure in a long black robe with a cap, standing at the other side of the room.

Opening my mouth I wanted to speak, but only a raspy sound came out. Immediately the figure turned around and I gasped. The hood covered most of his face, but I could see two burning red inhuman eyes looking at me.

He was next to me in a blink of an eye holding a glass of water. I took it gratefully gulping down the content. As soon as the water hit my throat it stung as if it had been ages since it had been lubricated.

When I was able, I spoke to the figure. "Who are you?"

My voice sounded weak and foreign to me as if I hadn't used it in a very long time.

"I am yours." The figure said. "I am your Grim Reaper. Assigned to your soul. Since you didn't die, I am tethered to you until you leave the mortal realm. I will do everything in my power to make sure that you will not die."

He sounded solemn as if he made me a vow, but I couldn't believe it. I raised my hand to the hood, needing to see his face to believe it. He let me pull down the fabric. When his face was uncovered, I gasped again and pulled my hand back.

He didn't have a face. He didn't have skin. I could see his skull as bright as day, as if someone had peeled off his flesh and muscles, and only left the carved-out remains of his head. The only thing that looked alive was his eyes. They were smoldering red coals deep inside the sockets. His mouth seemed as if it was fixed in a perpetual grin. His teeth were bare and pointy. He looked like death, and I guess he was.

I tried to wrap my head around it. Was this part of the curse?

"But why? How? What about all those people that died on my birthday?"

He looked away, playing with the hem of his black robe.

"That wasn't my assignment. I always kept an eye on you, but I couldn't interfere in what was happening."

"But why? Why? I need to know why? Am I cursed? What is it?"

My voice sounded shrill and hysteric. He put a finger on my lips to stop the words from coming out.

After a deep steading breath he said, "Yes and no. It isn't a curse exactly. It is a deal your parents made with the devil, and as he does he found a loophole."

"What deal?"

He shrugged. "I don't know the details but I knew it was about money."

I never knew my parents, but I couldn't imagine anyone making a deal for something so trivial as money. I had grown up with plenty, so maybe that is why it didn't seem as important to me. For all the people that I had lost, I had inherited money. I had more than I could ever think to spend, but it didn't make any sense. Shouldn't it have stopped after my family died? I didn't gain any money from losing a friend. Or did I? My thoughts raced a thousand miles per minute putting all the pieces together. I had gotten that promotion right after my work bestie died. And my best friend had left me her car that we bought together when we were 18.

I shook my head, not believing it. All this time I thought I was cursed, I had gained something from every single death.

"How can I fix it?"

He shook his head, not meeting my eyes. I grabbed his hand, feeling it warm and alive under mine. I wanted to stroke him, and feel more of him, but I needed to focus on what he wasn't giving me. He knew something he wasn't sharing and I needed to know.

"Tell me."

"By dying."

"Oh."

I loosened my grip on him. I had almost died, and I hadn't liked it. But maybe we could make it work. I was already thinking about the different ways I could escape death yet again.

"For how long do I need to be dead? Does it count if my heart stops and starts again? It could work. We could…"

He stopped my rant by gripping my hand. His hand felt so warm and big around mine. I enjoyed the feel of it, it made me feel grounded.

"I have just spent weeks trying to save you and you wish to die again?"

I shook my head with a smile. "Only for a minute or so. If we get the right equipment you can start my heart again."

I was already making a plan in my head, counting out the things we would need. For the first time in my life, I had hope again. Hope that I could break this curse, deal, whatever it was that was holding me back from living life to its fullest. I wouldn't have to be afraid of losing someone every year. I might even be able to try out having a relationship with someone. Having sex.

That thought stopped me in my tracks. I couldn't die a virgin. Weren't their rules against that kind of stuff? If I were to be sacrificed wouldn't the devil himself come to collect me as one of his brides?

I turned to look at my Grim Reaper again.

"I need to have sex first."

He almost choked in his surprise. He coughed and wheezed while I helpfully patted his back. He didn't feel bony underneath his robe at all. I could feel strong muscles working at his back while he tried to regain his breath.

"Hell, Lila. You're going to be the death of me."

I smiled at him. "Not if I die first." I shook my head, trying to get back to the subject at hand. "Look I don't want to die a virgin because Gods know what could happen then. So I need your help."

He stroked his chin with his hand deep in thought. "There has to be another way for this to work. We can't just."

I silenced him with a finger on his mouth. He had no lips, so I was touching his teeth, which felt kinda weird. How would it feel to kiss him? Did he have a tongue? He was speaking so he must have, but I hadn't seen it yet.

"You said you're my Grim Reaper. So who better to help me than you?" Suddenly a thought dawned on me and I took a step back. "Oh. Can you? I'm so sorry I didn't think. Anatomically speaking are you able to…"

I waved at his groin area instead of finishing my sentence. He growled at me. Like legit a full-blown animalistic monstrous growl. I could feel it vibrate through my body, and wetness seeped out into my panties.

His eyes burned brighter, and with one move he dropped his black robe. He was naked underneath it, and boy did he have the right anatomy for me. He was absolutely ripped. His muscular shoulders and his abs lead my eyes lower to his impressive cock that seemed to harden and grew as I looked at it.

It was massive, and when it reached its hardened state it looked like it was too big to fit. The only thing that hinted at him not being human was the color of his skin. It was the same color as his skull, an unnatural bony white that showed that his body was as monstrous as his face. The thing that impressed me the most was the ridges. I was pretty sure normal cocks didn't have those. They circled his cock like a spiral up to the tip. Immediately I wondered how those would feel inside of me.

"Can I touch it?" I asked, my voice a mere whisper.

He nodded once, and with his consent, I slid down on my knees before him. I was mesmerized by it. I lifted my hand, touching him carefully. His cock jumped up, and I let out a small gasp. Was that normal? I had never touched a cock and I didn't want to do it wrong. I looked up at him, biting my bottom lip trying to think of a way of asking him.

His eyes focused on my mouth and he groaned. "Whatever you will do it will be perfect Lila. Experiment and explore as much as you want."

That made my confidence grow. He didn't laugh at my inexperience, it even seemed to turn him on. I gripped it again and licked my lips wondering how he would taste. Another strangled groan sounded from above me and I smiled. He seemed to enjoy my touch so far.

I gripped him a bit tighter and marveled at his size. My fingers didn't even touch each other. How in the world would he fit inside of me?

He felt warm, throbbing, and alive underneath my touch. I stroked him up and down, enjoying the feel of the ridges beneath my palm. I twisted my hand, following the path of those ridges and I could feel him tremble beneath me. This creature, the Grim Reaper, bringer of Death was trembling beneath my fingers. I loved the surge of power and arousal coursing through me.

I leaned closer, sticking out my tongue to lick his tip. A strangled hiss escaped him. I loved the sound so I did it again and again. Licking at the tip of his cock, made him sound like a man overcome with desire. I explored the rest of him with my tongue, listening to the sounds he made.

My hands had been sitting still while I had focused on using my tongue. Now that I knew the feel of him, I wanted to experiment with both my hands and mouth at the same time. I gripped his cock, twisting my hand, and stroking along his ridges, while I sucked on his head simultaneously. It was enough to make him lose control. He snarled, and gripped my head, pulling me off him.

I protested, wanting to explore more of him, but before I knew it I lay in the bed beneath him. His big naked body covered mine. His eyes burned brighter than I had seen before and I trembled in anticipation.

"I need to have you now Lila before I lose control and cum like a teenager on a first date."

I moaned. "I want you to. Take me, fuck me, please."

In a flash, my clothes disappeared, and he was nudging his cock at my entrance. A hiss escaped me when I could feel him stretch me. He cursed and dove down between my legs. His tongue touched my pussy and I almost shot off the bed.

"You need to be nice and wet before I can fuck you," he murmured between licking me.

His tongue felt massive, long, and absolutely inhuman. I wanted to look down at what he was doing, but once he determined I was sufficiently wet, he was on top of me again.

"I need to fuck you now, Lila."

"Yes," I moaned. "Please fuck me, please."

In one push he was inside of me and I cried out with the pain and pleasure shooting through me. He held still inside of me, comforting me, stroking me, and murmuring sweet nothings in my ear.

"Short pain is better than drawing it out. I am sorry for hurting you, my sweet Lila."

I nodded, understanding why he did it. I never thought that losing my virginity would be pain-free, but after a short while, I could feel it ebbing away. With an experimental wiggle, I could only feel pleasure.

He took that as a sign that it was and pulled out. The ridges along his cock felt amazing pulling along the inside of my pussy. I moaned and clasped my legs around him, willing him to stay inside of me. When he pulled out almost all the way, he pushed back in, giving me that same amazing sensation. He did it again and again, finding an amazing rhythm that made me see stars.

I could feel the pleasure inside of me rising like a tidal wave. Sounds escaped me that I didn't even know I could make. Each pull and thrust felt better than the last and I knew it wouldn't be long before I would come. I squeezed my muscles around him, and he fucked me harder.

The pleasure grew and suddenly it snapped like a string. Waves of pleasure flooded my senses. My whole body trembled, my muscles squeezed him and I screamed out. I could feel his cock inside of me expand as he came as well, filling me with his cum.

He groaned and collapsed on top of me while tremors racked his body.

"I will do better next time," he murmured in my hair. "I will take my time to eat your pussy and make you cum all over my face."

"Oh wow. If that had been any better I think I might have died of pleasure."

A low chuckle sounded from him, and I realized I enjoyed hearing it. He sounded almost human at that moment. It felt like we were just two lovers, basking in the afterglow of our orgasm. But we weren't. He wasn't human, and we had a job to finish.

As soon as I was able I was going to sit up, but I just wanted to enjoy his warm embrace for a moment longer. He pulled off me, giving me the ability to breathe again, but I missed the warm comforting feeling of him. I turned and lay on his chest while his arms covered me.

When I felt that my heartbeat was back to normal I looked up at him. He was gazing at the ceiling lost in thought. I touched his bony cheek and his burning red eyes turned to me.

"Are you sure you want to go through with this Lila? You know I can keep you safe."

I shook my head. "I need to do this. If I don't I will be living the rest of my life scared to form any kind of connection out of fear of killing them. I want to live a normal life. Have normal relationships and be like any other person."

He stiffened beside me. "You want other relationships. I get it."

He nodded and got out of bed.

"I didn't mean it like that I..."

"No, you are right. I am just holding you back from living your life to the fullest."

I wanted to say something but suddenly he was gone, leaving me alone in the bed that was growing colder with the second now his body heat wasn't warning it anymore. As quickly as he had disappeared, he reappeared again, holding the equipment we needed.

"Let's get this over with, then you can go back to living your life, and I..."

He shook his head, not finishing his sentence. I wanted to say something, comfort him somehow, but I couldn't. Not yet. First I needed to get this over with before I lost my nerve. No more people would die for my benefit. This would end today.

He set up the equipment we needed and I laid down in the bed. The sheets still smelled like sex, and I wished we could just get in the bed again, and forget about my crazy idea. After a few deep steadying breaths where I focused on his scent, I nodded to him.

He looked at me with a grave look on his face. It was only a short while back that I had thought that the skull was terrifying and void of emotion, but now I could see multiple emotions cross his face. Anger, defeat, sorrow, and something that looked a lot like love. But it couldn't be, we only met a few hours ago.

Before I would lose my nerve, I closed my eyes, nodding one last time for him to do it, to kill me. He gave me an electric shock that stopped my heart, and I could feel my body shutting down. Darkness took over, and panic filled me. I didn't want to die, I wanted to live, and be with my Grim Reaper. My last thought of my feelings for him as I could feel myself drift away. A bright light greeted me and I floated to it...

Suddenly another shock brought me back. I could feel my heart beating, and I gasped, struggling to take in the air I needed to breathe. I was alive again. It had worked. I laughed and opened my eyes, looking straight into my Grims burning ones. A look of relief crossed his face, and before I knew it I was wrapped up in his arms. His face was buried in my hair.

"Oh, my dear Lila. Thank the Gods. I thought I had lost you," he murmured, rocking me gently against his body.

I welcomed his embrace, wrapping my arms around him as well. I was alive and I was horny.

"Fuck me," I moaned against his shoulder.

I stroked his trembling back, and arms, needing to touch him wherever I could.

"What?"

I pulled back and looked into his burning eyes. "Fuck me, please Grim. I need to feel alive. I need you inside of me. I need you."

His eyes burned brighter and before I knew it I was on my back, naked, and he was between my legs. He pushed into me, slowly this time, savoring the feeling of our joining. The urgency was gone, we could enjoy each other as if we had all the time in the world.

His cock felt amazing in me, the ridges blowing my mind yet again. They touched every pleasurable spot inside of me, even more, sensitive than the first time. My pussy fluttered around his cock, pulling him in deep with every thrust and trying to keep it inside with every pull.

"You feel so good inside of me," I moaned.

A full-body shudder racked through him and a guttural groan sounded from him.

"Fuck Lila you are perfect."

He fucked me harder and more urgently. I could feel my orgasm starting to rise, and I wanted him to join me. I squeezed my muscles around him, trying to keep him inside of me. Every pull and thrust felt more vibrant somehow. His thrusts grew in speed but lacked in accuracy. I could feel his cock starting to throb and expand and suddenly he came, filling me with his cum. The feeling of him coming inside of me ignited my own orgasm, and I screamed when the pleasure flooded my senses.

Before I was even done coming, he pulled out and dove down. I gasped when his tongue touched my sensitive pussy.

"I promised to eat you out until you cum all over my face," he mumbled.

He focused on his task and all rational thought left me. My body was still coming down from my previous orgasm when I could feel it getting ready for the next. Everything was sensitive and it didn't take long for his tongue to coax another climax out of me. It was smaller and warmer than the previous one, but still as pleasurable.

He fell down beside me and pulled me on top of him, his arms cuddling me close to him.

"Thank you," I said as soon as I was able to catch my breath again.

I lazily stroked circles in his chest hair, enjoying the feel of him next to me. His chest expanded and a deep sigh resounded from him.

"I need to go now," he said and I could hear the sorrow in his voice.

"What? Why? You said you were my Grim Reaper. That you were tethered to me."

"I was tethered to you because you didn't die, but since you died, my time is up, my tether is gone, and I need to go to my next soul."

I sat up, staring into his burning eyes. Those eyes that scared me first, made me feel safe now.

"You can't leave me. I need you. I…"

A finger on my lips silenced me. He shook his head.

"You need to live Lila. You are free to have normal relationships as you wanted, and I need to do my job."

"But I didn't mean romantic relationships. I meant friendships and going out with coworkers without fearing for their lives. I want you. I want a romantic relationship with you. I feel…"

My breath hitched as my throat closed up. My eyes burned and I fought off the tears as best as I could but one slipped out anyway. He touched my cheek, catching that one treacherous tear.

He looked at it with a wondering gaze.

"You want to be with me? A Grim Reaper. A bringer of death. A bad omen."

I nodded vigorously. I wanted that and so much more with him, but I didn't have the words for it. So I showed it with a kiss. I leaped up at him and kissed his skull everywhere. His teeth, his cheeks, his forehead, even around the glowing embers of his eyes.

He pulled me off him and I let my shoulders sag, defeated. He didn't want me the same way I did.

"There might be a way," he said.

I perked up, eager to hear what he had to say. He held my hand gently, looking deep into my eyes as if to search for something.

"If you stay with me, help me with my reaping we can be together. I only need to collect one soul a day, after that, we can spend time together however you want. I can provide for you, you don't need a job, we can just be happy together."

I gasped, there was a way we could be together but I would have to give up so much and be surrounded by death every day.

"Can I still have my own hobbies and friends?"

"Of course. You will still be human. Your friends won't be able to see me though, and I need to remain by your side at all times because as soon as you lose touch with me, I will disappear."

I nodded. I could do that. I had been surrounded by death all my life. I was pretty sure I could handle helping him with his work.

"I think we can make this work. At the very least we will try and see what happens next," I said with a smile.

He smiled back at me and gave me a kiss, my personal Grim Reaper, forever mine.

The End

Chased by the Werewolf

This was my first human - monster mixer, and I was feeling rather... to human to be here. Everyone was either gorgeous or monstrous, both equally attractive in their own way. I was just a run-in-the-mill average on all accounts human.

Maybe I should go back home? But I didn't have anyone or anything to go home to. That was why my cousin had pushed me to go to this monthly mixer. It matched up Monster and humans on the evening of the full moon to fuck. I really needed a good and hard fucking to just get my head sorted out and to be able to move on from my ex, who dumped me a few months ago because he didn't want children and I did.

I tried talking to a Minotaur and an Ogre, but there just wasn't any connection. I was attracted to monsters on a base level, but somehow I didn't see any of them screwing my brains out. With a sigh, I made my way to the exit to collect my things.

"You smell lost," I heard a delicious rough voice saying behind me.

As I turned around, I opened my mouth for a snarky comeback. The moisture left it and seeped right down into my panties when I got a good look at the creature the voice belonged to. Standing before me was a magnificent werewolf who was sniffing at me. His red and black checkered lumberjack shirt could barely contain his bulging muscles, and his jeans hugged his legs and package in the best way. I could see his furry tail wag behind him.

He was bending over to sniff at my hair with his gray-haired muzzle. His sharp teeth gleamed in the moonlight and when our eyes met, it was almost like an electrical spark coursed through me.

A feeling of connection, belonging, and warmth filled me with such a rush that it took my breath away.

"Hi," I almost moaned.

"Hi," he replied with a grin showing his teeth. "I have never smelled someone as delicious as you on one of these mixers."

Did I smell delicious? He looked delicious. If I had a spoon, I would just scoop him up. My brain seemed to work overtime while my mouth just hung open.

"I hope I am not being too forward, but would you like to be my partner for the nightly chase?"

When I didn't answer and just kept staring at him, he smiled again and continued.

"I'm a Werewolf and during the full moon, I go in heat and need to fuck and knot someone. In the olden days we would just pick whatever victim was close by, but these days we have these wonderful mixers that can pair us up with willing participants."

He waved around and I could see more couples pairing up. I had met no one that I even remotely had the same interest in, so I was all for his proposition. If my stupid mouth would just cooperate, I could accept.

"Me?" I managed to squeal.

The tone I produced was so high that I could see his pointy ears turn away. He barely contained a wince, but his enthusiastic smile didn't waver and his tail kept wagging.

"Yes, you."

He stuck out his massive paw, and I put my small hand in it. His hand felt soft and warm over mine. Another zing went through me with the touch and he growled. I quickly pulled my hand back as he coughed.

"Apologies," he said, while he readjusted his jeans and I could see a massive bulge threatening to break free.

"I'm forgetting my manners," he said with a wolfish grin. "My name is Mason. And you are?"

"Shay."

This time my voice sounded almost normal, but then he grabbed my hand again, made a bow, and kissed the top of it. I almost passed out because of the lack of oxygen in my brain and the fact that all the moisture in my body was now being redirected to my pussy.

"I would be honored to chase you tonight, Shay."

Another wordless sound escaped me, but that didn't deter him.

Mason winked at me and said, "Maybe after this, we can get a drink to get to know each other a bit."

A small laugh escaped me and I felt like I could breathe again. He was wonderful, trying to put me at ease while I was a mute mess.

"If you agree, we will get all the paperwork out of the way and check out compatibility. You won't have to worry about me getting you pregnant, but my heat will finish sooner if we are breeding compatible. You wouldn't want me fucking you all night, right?"

The idea of Mason fucking me all night was so hot that a small whimper escaped me. I wanted him to breed me, but I knew my birth control wouldn't let that happen tonight. But maybe in the future? I expelled the thought. I just met the guy, and I was already making plans that probably didn't even match up with him. He just needed someone to fuck during his heat, and I just needed to get fucked. This was just a pleasurable transaction. But maybe after that drink, something more could happen?

His huge paw on my shoulder took me out of my thoughts.

"Do you want to be my partner tonight, Shay?"

Oh, I hadn't even agreed yet. Of course, I wanted to.

"Yes," I said, glad that my voice sounded seminormal.

His grin widened and his face turned so handsome it took my breath away. I was really catching feeling for this Werewolf. He signaled to one of the organizers and before I knew it, I had the paperwork in front of me. I got tested, and it turned out we were almost 100% compatible. A little flutter in my stomach started when I heard that news.

Mason had given me some space to do all the paperwork, but my eyes kept drifting back to him. There was something about him that compelled my attention. I really hoped he would want to get that drink after if he wasn't disappointed by me.

After I went over all the legal and safety stuff, it was finally time for me to run. I could feel my heartbeat pick up, my breath came out in puffs, and my muscles clenched. I looked at Mason, who gave me an encouraging smile. Or at least I thought he was trying to look encouraging. He looked downright feral. His teeth gleamed in the dark with the saliva he was producing. His breathing was labored and I could see every single muscle tout ready to snap.

A shiver of delight went through me. I really was going to get chased and fucked by a monster. And not just any run-in-the-mill monster, no a full-blown Werewolf with the biggest dick I had ever seen.

My eyes zeroed in on the swinging appendage. He had gotten rid of his clothing and was now stark naked. I looked down at my light black summer dress. I wasn't too attached to it, and having him rip it off my body was bound to be incredibly hot. And I wasn't exactly ready to strip down in front of everyone.

I still couldn't believe I was doing this. If my cousin could see me now, she would probably cheer me on.

I focused back on his cock, since it was just hanging there. His gray fur covered his massive balls, but the rest of it was pink. Above his balls, there was a slight bulge I knew would expand when he knotted me. My eyes traveled higher over his impressive length, trying to calculate his grit. I knew it should fit since we were compatible but it still looked way too big to even enter me.

His tip was slightly curved and not mushroomed like the cocks I was used to, maybe that would help him slide inside of me. My muscles clenched at the thought. I might as well ditch my panties since they were so soaked they stuck to my pussy.

Mason was talking to someone who gave him a bottle. He accepted and thanked the person and started to rub the content of it on his dick. Oh god, he was lubing up. My insides clenched and I could feel more moisture seep out. I didn't think I needed lube, but it would probably help him later on.

A soft whimper escaped me while I watched him slather his cock in the lube. His head shot up and his eyes focused on me. His mouth widened in a predatory grin as he slowed his movements. He was giving me a show. Mason was telling me his dick was all mine with just his eyes, and I fucking loved every second of it.

A voice drew my attention, and one of the organizers approached me.

"We're ready if you are," she said with a smile.

After a last look back at Mason, who was still holding his cock, I nodded. With him not so close anymore, I finally regained the brain function to speak again.

"As ready as I'll ever be."

"You get a five-minute head start and when we blow the horn the second time, your match will leave. If at any time you want to stop you just have to say the word: Mixer, and a team will be on stand by to help you out. But don't worry," she said with a wink. "No one has ever complained about Mason."

Her words left a sour aftertaste in my mouth. How often did he do this? I was feeling a special connection all night, but for him was this just his monthly getaway to blow off some steam and to put his knot in someone? I didn't want to feel jealous, I just wanted to enjoy my evening. Straightening my back I ignored the turmoil inside of me. I was going to damn well enjoy myself.

I looked back at Mason, winked, and said, "Catch me if you can."

Before I could see his reaction, I ran off into the woods. His howls followed me into the dark. Since I didn't have night vision like some, I had been giving a substance on my hands that showed me the way. I held my hands outstretched when I ran to be able to see the path and to keep myself from running into the trees.

I ran as fast as I could. The muscles in my legs cramped up and my lungs burned. I definitely didn't have the physique for this kind of stuff, but it didn't matter, anyway. Before I knew it, I could hear a sound, and I knew he was following me. Instead of the horn, I was expecting, I heard an earth-shattering howl. In a matter of seconds, I could hear the forest around me go quiet.

The lack of sound was even more disconcerting than his howl had been. I slowed down, trying to find a place to hide or a tree to climb, when suddenly a rustle behind me made the hairs on my neck stand up straight. He was here, and he was watching me. Immediately I ran again, the feeling of being chased making me go faster than before, but there was no use in trying to run. Adrenaline and excitement coursed through me.

He toyed with me, guiding me with ease out into a clearing. Before I could turn around, he was on top of me. I was surrounded by him. The coarse hair on his chest rubbed at my back, his masculine, animalistic sweaty smell filled my senses and his growls filled my ears.

"I caught you," Mason growled in my ear.

He licked the shell of my ear with his big rough tongue, and I moaned.

"Now that I have caught you, I will fuck you, mark you, rut you, knot you, and mate you. You're mine."

My breathing stopped. We hadn't talked about mating. Mating was way more permanent than just fucking someone.

"Mating?" I asked, my voice a breathless whisper almost drowned out by the sounds of the forest surrounding us.

He licked the side of my neck, showing me the spot he had chosen.

"Only if you agree. You know the word if you want to stop."

I could feel his rock-hard, lubed-up cock rubbing at my ass and he was giving me the opportunity to think. If I hadn't already felt so strongly about him, those words definitely sealed the deal.

"Do it," I said.

A full-body shudder racked his body and his breathing became even heavier. I could feel him lift off and I almost whimpered in distress, but then he howled to the moon. The sound vibrated through the forest and I could feel it deep inside of me. He was letting the world know that he had found me and was going to claim me, and I loved it.

Mason ripped off my dress, threw it in front of me, and pushed my face into the fabric. Even in the heat of the moment, he was still being considerate of my comfort. If I hadn't been ready for this and dripping wet, that one movement should have sealed the deal on it.

His massive clawed paw was big enough to hold my entire head in its grasp. I tried to struggle, but all that resulted in was being pushed harder to the ground. He was bigger than me, stronger than me and I had nowhere to go. His free hand trailed down my naked back, leaving goosebumps in its wake. His claw snagged at the edge of my panties. With one movement, it was gone, ripped clean off my body.

A gasp escaped me, but it immediately turned into a moan when I could feel something wet touch my entrance. I held still, my whole body taut in anticipation, wondering what his next move would be. I could feel his body quiver. Incredibly slow he started to slide in, my pussy stretching to accommodate him.

I moaned, and he groaned in response, surging forward, impaling me on his dick. Mason filled me with one thrust, stuffing me full of his cock. My breathing came out in a whoosh. Never before had I felt so full in my life, but it was amazing. It felt like he touched every spot inside of my pussy that gave me pleasure.

With another guttural growl, he pulled back and thrust into me again. He pushed harder and fucked me to the ground, his balls slapping my clit with every thrust. He got into a maddening pace, claiming me with his cock like no one had ever done before.

Yes, this was just what I needed, a good and hard monster fuck. Who needed therapy when they could just get their brains and worries fucked out?

Pleasure rose as he rubbed my inner walls with his cock. It felt like the best massage in the world, releasing me from all my stress and worries. I let myself float on the high he was giving me, just feeling pleasure and not thinking about anything but his massive cock filling me.

"You're mine," he growled in my ear as he fucked me hard.

The paw that held me down on the ground slid forward. One of his fingers grazed over my clit. My body pushed up, but I didn't get far with his gigantic form covering me. More pleasure filled my senses as he strummed my clit while he fucked me. His hot breath in my ear made shivers pass through me as he growled filthy things.

"I'm going to fill you with my cum. My knot will make sure none of it goes to waste. Then I will mark you as mine."

His tongue slid back over the spot on my shoulder where I knew he would sink his teeth in. His rhythm never wavered. Anticipation and pleasure surged through me. I hadn't expected to find him, but somehow it was perfect. This entire experience was perfect. Feeling his colossal body on mine, his cock inside of me. Smelling the green of the woods mixed with his sweaty, animalistic scent. Hearing his rough voice, grunts, and growls in my ear. All of it combined made me feel special and cherished by him.

"I'll fuck you again and again until you're filled with my pups."

A whimper escaped me at the mention of having children with him. I would love to create a family with him. I could already imagine little wolf children running around Mason laughing and growling playfully. My heart squeezed and a warm feeling filled me. It was probably the heat or the mating frenzy speaking, but I loved every word that came out of his mouth.

"The moment you ran, I knew you were mine. They couldn't even hold me for the mandatory five minutes," Mason growled. "You're mine, Shay, forever."

I moaned in response. Words escaped me yet again, but it didn't matter. My body responded for me. I could feel my muscles clamp down on his cock, triggering my orgasm. Waves of pleasure washed over me as my body grew rigged, my pussy muscles milking his cock. Another howl escaped him as Mason came as well. He filled me with his seed, prolonging my pleasure.

Just when I thought I would shatter from the pleasure inside of me, I could feel him push deeper into me and start to expand. I had almost forgotten about his knot, but it made its presence known in the best way. His knot stretched my pussy to the max capacity, trapping his seed inside of me and the both of us together. A sigh escaped me as the tension escaped my body and only pleasure and love remained. Little tremors of pleasure racked my body as he moved closer.

"I'll mark you now," he whispered in my ear.

His voice was soft and caring, the breeding urgency the heat gave him gone. He licked me again on my shoulder, creating another shiver. Mason moved the paw that held my head down and grabbed my neck as he held my shoulder with the other.

"It will only hurt for a moment. Don't fight it," he said.

Before I could reply, he sunk his teeth into me and it felt like a fire had entered my body. A strangled cry escaped me, but almost immediately the pain turned into something warmer. A feeling of love, belonging and companionship filled me and I realized the mating bond must have formed between us.

Pleasure pushed forward, and another sudden orgasm washed over me. I moaned and I could feel him come as well. He pulled his teeth out and licked the wound, grumbling content as he did. His cock pulsating, his seed filling me, trapped by his knot.

"You're mine now and I'm yours."

"I love you," I blurted out.

Before I could regret the words, Mason nuzzled my cheek and said, "I love you, too. As soon as my knot is gone, I'm going to turn you around and fuck you again. Then I'm taking you home and treating you to that drink I promised."

That sounded perfect to me. I hadn't expected it to, but going to this mixer had been the best decision of my life.

The End

Trapped with the Yeti

This was not my idea of a fun vacation. I was hiking behind a Yeti twice my size that took one step for every three steps that I took. If my best friend Evelyn hadn't just had an adorable baby with her Yeti husband and granted me the honor of being godmother I would not be here.

But here I was, in the snow, using my last vacation days to do a two-day hike to the cave she lived in. I still couldn't believe that she actually lived in a cave. The few times she came to the town nearby and was able to contact me she had told me it was cozier than it sounded and she did appear happy.

If her Yeti husband looked anything like my guide I could understand her being happy. I stared at his massive back, the white fur covering it looking soft. My fingers itched to caress it to see if he was as cuddly as he looked. His delicious backside was only covered by a short to hide his modesty.

The only issue with Seth, my Yeti guide, was that he appeared to have a disdain for humans. The moment we met his eyes had darkened and he hadn't looked happy to have to help a tiny human like me through the mountains.

I had tried to start a conversation but his one-word grunted responses had left me irritated. It didn't help that he was gorgeous, and I was attracted to him while he obviously disliked me. I had always had a thing for monsters, dating several in my past, but never before had I met anyone as attractive as Seth. His piercing blue eyes and gorgeous white soft fur made me almost drool. It really wasn't fair that the best monsters kept to themselves and lived in the mountains. If he ever came to the city, women would flock around him.

I didn't know why that idea bothered me. After he dropped me off at my friend's cave I wouldn't even see him again. But there was something about him, that I couldn't really put my finger on.

"I'm tired," I sighed when the sky darkened and I could feel my legs tremble with fatigue.

He grunted, shaking his head. "No Alice. We need to keep going. Storm coming."

His deep rumbling voice with his delicious accent hugged me, but as soon as his words registered my mood soured. This might have been more words than he had said to me during the entire trip but I was sick of it.

I stopped, crossing my arms. "No."

He turned around, his vibrant blue eyes shooting daggers at me. "What?"

"No," I said. "My forecast said it won't storm. I'm tired and Evelyn said it was a two-day hike. We need to stop for the night and continue tomorrow."

"Where? No hotel around," he said, waving his hand around.

"Evelyn said that there are travel caves around. Take me to one of those for the night to sleep and we will continue tomorrow," I said not relenting.

I was hungry, tired, and sore. I had walked more this day than I had in the past year and I was not going to let some bossy Yeti order me around.

He growled at me like an actual animal, shook his head, and then sighed. "Fine. Next travel cave an hour that way," he said and started walking to the right.

I had no choice but to trust his word and follow him, hoping to get a place to sleep for the night. I was already regretting the second bag I had brought with me, feeling my shoulders ache with the weight of it.

Within the hour we arrived at the cave which was surprisingly cozier than I had expected. It was stocked like a basic vacation cabin with a large Yeti-sized bed, a little kitchenette, and even an improvised bathroom type of situation. I cleaned myself up the best I could, changed into my pajamas, and was happy to see that Seth had started warming up some soup.

I gratefully accepted the food and we ate in silence. After my belly was full and I had warmed myself to the fire Seth had made, I studied him. He was quite handsome. I was still shocked that my best friend had married a Yeti, but seeing Seth in all his brooding silence, big, strong, and hairy kinda did things to my lady parts that had been dormant for a while. And I had to admit that the baby of Evelyn and Jens was the cutest little ball of fur in the whole world. I had only seen some pictures and I couldn't wait to hold my godchild in my hands.

Out of habit I took out my phone and groaned when I saw that I had no reception. I got the whole hot Yeti cute baby thing but I didn't understand how someone could live so disconnected from the world. My fingers already itched to look up the news, weather report, social media, whatever to just not have to listen to the silence of the cave. I grew up in the city and the silence of nature always gave me chills. I hoped I was going to be able to sleep tonight, but feeling the physical toll this day had taken on me, I was pretty sure I would fall asleep fast.

I stretched, yawned, and said, "Welp, I'll go to sleep then. See you tomorrow."

I started walking towards the bed.

"What do you think you are doing," Seth asked and stood up taking a step towards the bed as well.

I took another step and said, "Going to bed."

He shook his head and went to the bed. "I take the bed, you sleep on the mat."

"What? I'm a guest and I should..."

"I am bigger so I take the bed. Tiny humans like you can curl up anywhere. I need to be able to stretch out."

I gasped in outrage. Did he just compare me to a cat? Like a human didn't need to have some comfort to be able to sleep.

"What is your deal with humans anyway? You have been a dick all day."

He stepped closer to me, and I could feel the warmth radiating from him. I wanted to punch him and snuggle closer to him at the same time.

"You are too tiny and weak. I don't get why anyone would be attracted to you. It would never fit."

"What would never fit?"

"My cock."

I gasped my eyes shooting lower to his loose shorts that barely contained the bulge he was sporting. Of course, he was handsome, an asshole, and had a big dick. But if I knew one thing, it was that humans and Yetis were compatible.

"That is ridiculous," I said. "Evelyn and Jens have managed just fine."

He huffed annoyed and crossed his arms. "Mine is bigger than Jens."

I got distracted for a moment looking at his bulging biceps, but when his words registered I choked out a laugh. Had he measured both? Or was it a Yeti thing to know about the size of everyone's cock? Gods, I was too tired to argue and I just wanted to sleep. I patted his arm, reveling in the soft feel of his fur.

"Sure it is big guy. I'm going to sleep."

I crawled into the bed before he could protest. I yawned and motioned to the other side. "Plenty of room for both of us even with your big dick energy."

He grumbled something but got in the bed behind me. His warmth immediately surrounded me and before I knew it I had dozed off.

I WOKE UP, FEELING groggy and cold. I looked around me and saw Seth standing in the entryway brooding like he had done the day before. I stretched out and made a moaning sound that attracted his attention.

His stormy gaze locked on my face and he snarled, "Look. Your forecast was wrong. Now we are trapped here for another day."

Still sleepy, and with a morning temper that went right to cranky without my morning coffee I shot up out the bed and marched over to him.

I poked at his chest and said, "Because you were right about this, doesn't mean you're right about everything."

I had it with this asshole of a Yeti thinking he was better than me and knew everything.

"I am. I was right about the storm and I am right about humans. You are weak and tiny and..."

I cut off his words effectively by grabbing him by the balls. I was sick and tired of him being an asshole. I knew for a fact that humans could take big dicks and he was no exception.

"I will fucking prove to you that you're wrong," I gritted out between my teeth.

I pulled down his boxer, releasing his colossal cock. It was magnificent, pink, hard, and bigger than my forearm. For a moment a tinge of worry filled me. He was absolutely massive, but I knew I could make it work. I bend down and before he could even protest I took the tip of his dick in my mouth.

"Wh... What are you doing?" Seth groaned.

I released his dick with a plop and licked my lips. His blue eyes sparkled with passion, and I couldn't hold back my grin.

"Proving that a tiny human like me can take your big Yeti cock," I said.

Before he could reply, I put my mouth on his cock again. He growled, and I could feel his gigantic body tremble. I sucked on the tip, loving the taste of his precum. It had a salty and musky flavor to it that made me want to drink all of it.

I grabbed his length with my hands and started to stroke him with sure and steady movements. Both my hands were just big enough to encompass him. His girth was frightening and arousing at the same time. How would it feel inside of me?

I couldn't fit a lot more than the tip but I made sure that the rest of his cock was thoroughly pleasured as well. I kept stroking his length with one hand as I slide the other one down between his legs. His balls were covered in the same soft fur as his body and felt heavy and warm in my hand. I couldn't fit both in my hand, so I massaged them individually dividing my attention between them.

His scent surrounded me as I worked over his cock. The animalistic, masculine, husky smell of him, made my own desire grow. The sounds he was making became more and more feral as he voiced his pleasure. Growls, grunts, and moans alternated and I loved every one of them.

The big bad Yeti was at my mercy and I could feel his giant body tremble with desire. I was getting aroused feeling him lost in his pleasure. As I looked up I could see that he had closed his eyes and his face was contorted with bliss. His massive hands were clasped in fists by his side and I saw that he barely contained himself. I wanted him to lose control. I needed him to surrender to the pleasure I was giving him to prove I was right.

I increased the pressure and speed of my ministrations on his cock as I sucked with all my might on his tip. I felt him vibrate and his balls tighten. A shiver went through his body and I could feel him starting to come before his seed hit my tongue. I swallowed it down greedily as he shouted out his release. He came so much that some of it dripped out over my chin. Before I could say anything, he gripped me, pulled me into his embrace, and walked over to the bed. His soft fur caressed my skin, and I reveled in the warmth he was emitting.

"You're mine now, Alice," he growled before he dropped me.

My body was humming with arousal and his taste still lingered in my mouth. My brain tried to catch up, but he had already ripped off my pajama. His big hands grabbed my thighs and pushed them apart. His head dived in between my legs and I moaned as he started to lick my pussy. His tongue was massive and I could feel pleasure course through my body. It was twice the size of my hand, and with every lick, he touched every pleasure point surrounding my pussy.

"You took my seed, and now you will take my cock," he growled when he came up for air.

He dove back down and distracted me with so much pleasure that I still couldn't react. What had he said? I was his? I hadn't agreed to anything, but boy did I want to take his cock.

My muscles squeezed around nothing and I moaned. I was so wet and his tongue was pushing me to the brink so fast that I could barely catch up. He used his thumbs to spread open my pussy lips to be able to reach more of me.

He curled up his tongue, surrounding my clit. He stimulated the sensitive bud and when he started to suck I lost it. My orgasm washed over me in pleasurable waves. I cried out, my back arching off the bed as tremors racked my body.

Before I could catch my breath he already loomed over me. His arms caged me in, and his massive body blocked out the light and our surroundings. All I could see was him, all I could smell was the scent of our mixed desire and all I could feel was his soft fur caressing my body. I lifted my hand, cupping his cheek.

His eyes had an intense look to them. The blue in them sparkled and even with the tremors of my orgasm still shaking my body, I had a feeling this was more than just a fuck. I wanted to ask him, but words left me as I felt his cock at my entrance.

I looked down and saw his massive Yeti cock presented at my pussy. It looked almost comically large but I knew I could take him. I opened my legs wide, gripped his shoulders for leverage, and lifted up my hips as a sign for him to continue. With a growl, he slowly pushed inside. After a little resistance, my pussy relaxed and he slid inside.

My breath came out in a woosh as he filled me up with more and more of his cock. It felt like he went on forever and filled me to the brink. His cock stroked my inner walls, stretching me to be able to accommodate him. Just when I thought I couldn't take more of him, he bottomed out. His hips met mine and he was fully inside of me.

"Told you it would fit," I managed to gasp.

He pulled out and thrust back in, touching me in all the right places. His massive cock stretched my pussy and it burned in the most delicious way. Each thrust was smoother, aided by our combined juices.

"You take my cock. You're mine," he growled.

His face contorted with pleasure, his sparkling blue eyes were filled with so many emotions that I couldn't recognize all of them. His hips pumped against mine as his dick fit inside of me perfectly.

"What?" I gasped.

I gripped the fur on his shoulder tighter, needing something to hold onto as he gave me the fucking of a lifetime.

"Yetis breed for life. I will breed you and you will be mine forever."

So by fucking him I had agreed to be his wife? That was what having a big mouth got you, trapped with a Yeti. While he thrust into me again and pleasure-filled my senses I realized I didn't mind it. My best friend had the cutest Yeti baby and a loving husband, so why shouldn't I enjoy what was happening? I let all rational thoughts and issues about the practical side of things go and surrendered to the pleasure he was giving me.

"Breed me, Seth," I moaned, as I wrapped my legs around him spurring him on.

He gripped my hip with one of his massive hands, angling me in a way that made his cock touch my g-spot. Sparks burst behind my eyes and I could feel myself racing to the finish line.

"I will fill you with my seed and breed yeti babies in you, Alice," he growled as he fucked me harder.

I exclaimed my agreement as the pleasure inside of me grew. Each thrust took me higher and I knew it wouldn't be long before I came. I touched him wherever I could, loving the feel of his soft fur beneath my hands. Sounds of desire and pleasure left me as he growled out his own pleasure.

After another thrust, pleasure flooded my senses. My muscles squeezed around his cock as my whole body spasmed with my release. I cried out, my voice filling the cave, as wave after wave of pleasure washed over me. He growled, thrust into me two more times, and then I could feel him come as well. His seed filled me, and warmth spread inside of me. He trembled on top of me, his arm keeping him upright so as not to crush me.

After another breath, he rolled us over, embracing me in his arms, and closing me in. I lifted my hand to his cheek again, cupping it, stroking my thumb over his lips. He closed his eyes and I felt his whole body vibrate as the last of his seed left him.

"We haven't even kissed yet," I whispered, suddenly feeling my voice was too loud for the intimate moment we shared.

He opened his eyes, a swarm of emotions filling in the blue. He leaned closer and our lips met. I opened my mouth and moaned. His tongue met mine in a passionate dance. His unique taste was mixed with the taste of my desire and I loved it. He growled and deepened the kiss.

His arms around me, gripped me tighter and he hugged me close to his chest. I felt cherished and safe in his embrace. His words during our lovemaking played around in my head. I might not have intended to create a bond between us with sex, but it had happened. He might be a grump with big dick energy, but as of this moment, he was my grumpy yeti.

Our kiss broke off as we both gasped for breath, but we held each other close.

"You're mine," I mumbled, kissing his cheeks, forehead, and anywhere on his face that I could reach.

"All yours," he said. "And you're mine, Alice."

I came to visit my best friend and God Child and I had found a Yeti husband. My vacation ended up being a lot more fun than I had imagined.

The End

A Mate for the Vampire Queen

I am the Vampire Queen. I have been alive for hundreds of years, and I am the oldest living creature in this hemisphere. The mere whisper of my name made men, monsters, and animals tremble in fear, but this wolf just looked at me with a challenging gaze.

Not even an Alpha. A mere Beta captured in my territory. He should beg for mercy on his knees, squeal like a pig, weep and moan, but all he did was stare at me. I always enjoyed a challenge, but when you get to be my age, it all seemed trivial after a while. His gaze made me feel alive for the first time in a hundred years, and I wasn't sure if I enjoyed the feeling.

"Why is he here?" I asked.

"He said that…"

"He can speak for himself," the Wolf interrupted one of my court people. "I'm Isaac, Beta to Luna Cassidy of the Nightwind pack. I have a message from your Vampire Elijah. I need to convey it to you in private."

He dipped his head in the smallest sign of respect I had ever seen, but respectful nonetheless. I laughed out loud. The screeching sound filled my throne room. As a ploy to try to get me alone, it was a good one. My trusted adviser had disappeared two weeks ago, and I knew he had sensitive information on him. They either killed him or held him somewhere captive.

Either way, I wanted to know what happened to him. I had no fear that I couldn't take this Wolf in a battle if the need arose. I dismissed my court, curious to see what he would do. It had been a while since someone challenged me in this way.

As soon as the last of my people left, I waved my hand at him.

"Speak. And do so quickly. I do not have the patience for a long-winded story about how you sniffed something."

He snorted and wiggled his hands. "I might speak faster if not held back by these chains."

Another laugh escaped me. As if I would release him of his bounds when alone. I knew I could take him, but I didn't much feel for killing today. This wolf had made me laugh more than most of my minions had in a decade. It could be quite refreshing having an animal at court. Maybe I should see on taking a pet when this pesky war was over.

When the Wolf noticed I had no intention of heading his request, he sighed.

"Fine. I guess I can speak like this." His easygoing demeanor disappeared and his voice became grave. "The Vampire Elijah has mated to my Luna. With the information he had, we propose a truce between our people."

Another laugh escaped me. Two jokes in one go. A mating between a Vampire and a Wolf and a truce between our people? He was a madman. I was ready to summon someone to take him away when he continued.

"The Gargoyles have closed an alliance with the Nagas and are planning an attack. We know that once they have taken you out, we will most likely be the next target. Those two species together can take either of us from the ground and the air, but if we work together, we might be able to come to a standstill without too much bloodshed."

I mulled over his words. I knew the Gargoyles had been vying for my territory for a while, but I never expected them to band together with the Nagas.

"How do I know you aren't lying?"

"Taste my blood. Aren't you the mystical Vampire Queen that can taste if someone is being truthful or not? Elijah told me."

I took a step closer and his delectable scent hit my nostrils. My skill wasn't common knowledge. I had used it to my advantage many times and it would lose some of its value if my enemies would know of it.

"What if you took poison to get rid of me?"

He chuckled. "That would fuck me over as well, and I'm honestly way too happy living life and looking for my Mate."

His Mate. For some strange reason, those words awoke something inside of me. Not sure what it was, I buried it deep to focus on the situation at hand. Tasting him.

In one movement, I stood beside him. He smelled, unlike any Wolf I had ever met before. They usually smelled like wet dogs and dirt, but his scent was delicious. Like a mixture of dark coffee, chocolate, and the highest-quality whiskey. His scent alone would be enough to make me drunk even if I couldn't anymore. I had to focus, not imagine getting drunk on a Wolf. Leaning closer, my nose almost touched his neck, and took a deep whiff. I couldn't detect any poison beneath that delectable aroma.

Without another thought, I sunk my fangs into his neck. Our groans filled the empty room. Mine was from utter bliss and his? I didn't know, and I didn't care. All I could think about was his taste exploding in my mouth. His blood was the deepest, richest, most delicious thing I had ever drank in all my afterlife.

There was a definite quality difference between humans and all monsters, with virgins being on top of the list. But I doubted this fine specimen of a man would be a virgin. He tasted even better than he smelled, like all the things I missed about being human. It has been so long that I almost didn't remember it, but the joy of experiencing new tastes was one of those things that I missed.

I drank more and more, guzzling it up as if it was my own personal landline to feel human again. He made sounds that could be pleasure, but I was so focused on my fulfillment that I almost didn't hear them. Places in my body awoke that had been dormant for some time. My pussy throbbed in the same rhythm as his heartbeat. I might be able to come from just drinking him and listening to his moans. It was when his sounds died out, and his heartbeat slowed down that I regained my sanity again. It was one of the hardest things I had done in a long time, but I retracted my fangs from his neck before I killed him.

I felt like a newly turned vamp, not able to stop when feeding. It appalled me, but as the queen that I was, I didn't let it show on the outside. I summoned my minions to take him to a regeneration room to get him back up to strength. I hesitated and almost added that they should treat him with care, but I didn't. With this war looming closer than I had anticipated, I couldn't show weakness.

With his vital blood pumping through me, I felt more alive than I ever had, and I needed to come up with a strategy. I called upon all of my advisers and we send out spies to check the truth of his statements.

Before I knew it, a week had passed, and I hadn't drunk any more blood. Usually, I fed every day or so just to keep my strength up, but after tasting Isaac's blood, I hadn't felt like drinking any other. I could survive without blood for years, so I didn't need to drink so often. Somehow all I could think about was the taste of my Wolf's blood in my mouth.

I went back to my chambers, almost too distracted to notice someone in them. As soon as I closed the door, I could feel the hairs on my neck stand up straight. I whirled around just in time to stop Isaac from grabbing me. He stopped a hairbreadth away from my face, panting angrily. I was a tall woman, usually a head taller than most humans I met, but he stood higher than me. I had to tilt my neck slightly to look into his eyes. They burned bright green with anger and I could see flickers of brown as his Wolf was trying to take over.

"You left me," Isaac growled.

I opened my mouth to answer, but he stopped me with another growl.

"You drank me half to death and then left me. How could you do that to your Mate?"

"Mate?" my voice sounded shrill in my own ears. How could he think I was his Mate?

Isaac took a step closer, so we were nose to nose. "Yes, your fucking Mate. Don't you dare deny it. I know that you have tasted me and cannot resist another taste."

My Wolf bent his neck to the side, offering his delectable throbbing artery up as a meal. I licked my lip, unable to resist. His delicious scent consumed me and I knew that tasting him would be even better. I craved his blood on my tongue. I needed it so badly, but I had to have self-restraint. With a hiss, I backed away, but he just followed me until my back was against the door. His hot, muscular body pushed close to me. His warmth and his scent enveloped me like a blanket.

"Taste me again to see the truth in my words."

The truth? I had forgotten to check it somehow. I had just trusted his words and started out my campaign based on his claims. They had turned out to be real, but still. I never let my emotions run me around, but he had me wrapped around his finger without even trying. One taste had been enough for me to trust him.

Maybe I should taste him again to find out if what he was saying was true? Any excuse to taste him was enough. His luscious, delectable scent surrounded me as he inched his neck closer. I could hear his heartbeat speed up, and I knew he wanted this as much as I did. My fangs almost hurt from the anticipation as I surrendered to the pull he had on me.

I sunk my teeth into his neck and moaned as his delicious taste hit my tongue. He tasted even better than I remembered. I gripped his shoulders to keep me steady and loved the way his muscles tensed underneath my touch. Isaac pushed his firm, hot body closer to mine as he growled into my ear.

"Taste me, and admit that I'm your Mate."

My thoughts and senses were all jumbled up, but I could taste the truth in his words. He was my Mate. Somehow, through the weirdest way the universe worked, his Moon Goddess had chosen me to be his Mate. His taste filled my every sense and pleasure coursed through me. There was nothing in the world that came even close to being as delicious as his blood. My body heated up with his life essence flowing through me. My pussy throbbed and I could feel wetness seeping out.

I moaned and opened my legs to steady my stance. He immediately pushed one of his muscular thighs in between, giving me just the right amount of friction that I needed. My body reacted on instinct. As I drank his blood like a starved woman, I ground down on his legs, chasing my orgasm. Isaac grabbed my hips to guide the pace. The rhythmic push and pull felt amazing on my pussy. The pleasure inside of me grew with every suck and every touch on my clit.

I pulled my fangs out in time with my orgasm flowing through me. Waves and waves of pleasure washed over me as a hoarse, pleasured cry left me. My legs trembled as his powerful arms held me upright. I felt calm for the first time in eons, realizing that I had my Wolf, my Isaac, here with me.

Loneliness was a strange thing when you got to be my age. It somehow crept up on me when more and more people I knew were just gone one day. Seasons, countries, and economics changed, but I stayed the same through all of it, alone. But now Isaac was here as my Mate and I never had to be alone again.

I gazed into his beautiful green eyes and saw my emotions reflected in them.

"Do you believe me now, my Mate?" Isaac asked in an unbelievably tender voice.

Not trusting my own voice, I just nodded. We were Mates, now and forever. But that meant that I had a weakness. If word got out that the Vampire Queen was Mated to a Wolf, none of my enemies would stop before he was gone. I pushed him away, averting my gaze. I couldn't look at him or I would drown in those puppy eyes.

"Guards," I yelled.

Immediately, my room was filled with my most loyal subjects. Before Isaac could even react, he was collared, chained, and muzzled. He tried to break free, but the silver that we used was of the purest quality.

"Take him to our location no one can find."

Isaac's eyes turned dark and feral. Maybe he had heard the stories about it? People and monsters often disappeared in my territory to never be found again. I would do the same thing to him, but only to keep him safe. I steeled my heart, not able to look at him when they took my struggling Mate away.

It took him exactly three days to escape and find me again. He stormed into my council meeting in Wolf form and almost killed two of my personal guards before I raised my voice.

"Everyone out!"

Every single person in the room obeyed, except, of course, my Wolf. As soon as the room was empty Isaac turned into his human form again, still growling angrily. His naked form was covered with blood and dirt, and yet he never looked more beautiful than at this right moment.

"Are my guards' death?" I asked.

My voice sounded calmer than I felt. Inside of me, a turmoil of emotions were waging war. Happiness at seeing him again, anger at his disobedience, hunger for his blood, and lust all fought for their place. In the end, hunger and lust won when Isaac marched over to me and kissed me.

His lips were like fire beneath mine, burning away any lingering doubt I had about our bond. Isaac was a worthy Mate. If he could fight off ten of my best people, he would be able to stand on his own against my enemies.

"You're mine," he growled against my lips.

I pulled my head away, looking into his eyes. They were filled with so many emotions it was hard to pinpoint. But I couldn't just ignore his claim.

"I am the Vampire Queen. I belong to no man."

"You're my Queen, my Mate, my beloved," Isaac said as he pulled me closer. "I'll bow for you, worship you. I would even die for you because you're mine. We are Mates, we are equal. I'm yours and you're mine."

His words awoke something inside of me that I hadn't felt in a very long time. Long before I became a Vampire I had loved a man once, but never were those feelings as strong as these.

I kissed him again in a frenzy. Our teeth clashed, our lips mashed, and a drop of blood escaped his lip.

I sucked it up and moaned. "I need to taste you again."

Immediately, he shifted his head, so I had clear access to his neck. His heartbeat was going a thousand miles a minute and his artery was throbbing seductively. I didn't waste a second and sunk my fangs into his neck. His familiar delicious taste filled my mouth as his scent filled my nose. My scenes were surrounded by him. I needed just a taste to acknowledge his claim about me. Isaac was mine, and I was his in every way possible.

My pussy was throbbing in time with his heartbeat. As soon as my teeth left his neck, he positioned me on top of the table. Important documents surrounded us, but I only had eyes for him.

"Now it's my time to taste you," Isaac growled.

He ripped off my gown, and I lay naked before him as an offering. Spreading my thighs, I smelled my arousal in the air. He closed his eyes, growling, and I could see how he was trying to gain control again. I didn't want him in control, I wanted him crazy with need for me. I pushed a hand down, spreading my pussy lips for him. Isaac opened his eyes, threw his head back, and howled to the Moon Goddess. A second later, he was on my pussy, devouring me as if he wanted to remember my taste forever.

He used his lips, tongue, and teeth to get me to my release faster than anyone had before. His blood was pumping through me as his touches pushed me higher and higher. I gripped his hair, needing something to hold on to as he rocked my world. The silky soft strands tickled my fingers while he devoured my pussy. When I felt it would take only the smallest push to send me over the edge, he stopped. His eyes locked onto mine as he licked his lips in the most sensual way.

"Mate," Isaac growled, low and dangerous. "Say that I am your Mate."

His eyes flicked between vibrant green, and dark brown as his Wolf tried to take over. He looked feral, magnificent, and beautiful. All mine.

"My Mate," I moaned and immediately he latched onto my pussy again.

The pleasure inside of me grew with each lick, suck, and nip. Soon it was too much for me and the dam broke. Wave after wave of pleasure washed over me, as I screamed out his name. Isaac rumbled happily against my pussy, the vibrations only adding to my climax. My whole body trembled with the release as pleasure filled my every sense. The orgasm left me feeling invigorated.

"Now it is my turn again," I said and pushed him up against the wall.

I got down on my knees in front of him, reveling in his amazing naked form. I was in a submissive position in front of him, but gripping his rock-hard cock, I knew I had all the power. A hiss escaped him, as I grabbed his hard length firmer. He was as strong as me, so I didn't need to be afraid of breaking him. My fingers couldn't encompass him whole. He was marvelous, delicious, and impressive. His would be my first and last Wolf cock and I loved every inch of it.

Without any further teasing, I put my mouth on his cock. I licked and sucked on the tip and then pulled him into my awaiting mouth. He was massive, but I knew how to deal with big cocks. I pushed him past my throat, ignoring my gag reflex until all of him was engulfed by me. My nose hit his pelvis as I bobbed my head. The pleasurable, primal sounds that escaped him made me enjoy this even more. He wasn't afraid to voice his desire, and I loved hearing it. Every movement of my tongue elicited another delicious sound.

"Fuck, your mouth feels amazing."

His grunted praise meant more to me than any compliment I had ever received. I wanted him to lose control and only ever think of me. I pushed my head down again, swallowing all of him as I grabbed his thighs, scratching him lightly. His whole body trembled, and I could feel his climax approaching. I swallowed again, loving the feel of him in my throat.

I tilted my head a bit and one of my fangs scraped the side of his cock. A drip of blood escaped, and I moaned, reveling in his taste. Isaac growled and came without a warning. His cum filled my mouth and mixed in with the lingering taste of his blood. It was the most delicious cocktail I had ever drank. I pulled back and swallowed every last drop of his release. After I had licked all of it off his cock, he was still amazingly erect. I cocked an eyebrow, and he smiled a predatory smile back.

"Werewolf Stamina, my Mate. I can go all night."

"Perfect. Me too," I said.

Isaac pulled me up and kissed me again. Our tastes mingling, the scent of our release heavy in the air. He put me on the table again, but I stopped him.

"My chambers," I said as I nibbled on his ear.

Isaac grabbed me, and in a flash, we were on my bed. He threw me on it and I almost giggled as I bounced on my mattress. I had never giggled before, but somehow this Wolf made me do things I never thought I would.

He dove between my legs, licking my pussy like a starved man. "I need to taste you again," Isaac growled. He licked me and moaned. "By the Moon Goddess, you're the best thing I ever tasted. I could stay down here forever."

My cheeks heated up and as I lay my hands on them, I noticed I was blushing. With his blood coursing through me, my body was responding in ways it hadn't before. I also needed another taste, but there was something else that I needed even more.

"Fuck me, Isaac, and Mark me."

He growled, continuing his assault on my pussy. My back bent off the bed, pleasure shot through my body and I was almost ready to come again. His talented mouth brought me pleasure and before I knew it my orgasm took over. Waves of pleasure washed over me as my body trembled with my release. My muscles tightened around nothing, and I needed to be filled by him.

I flipped us over, straddling him. "Mark me," I said as I let his rock-hard cock slip inside of me.

Our pleasured sounds mingled until the room was filled with them. He filled me perfectly, touching every pleasure point that existed inside of me. I closed my eyes to be able to enjoy the sensation of his amazing cock inside of me. He thrust up, giving me even more pleasure.

"The strongest Mating Bonds are forged during the height of our pleasure," Isaac growled as he fucked me.

I rode him hard and quickly, determined to get us there as fast as possible. Our bodies were moving in sync as we climbed higher and higher. His hands covered my breasts and pinched my nipples, only enhancing my pleasure. It wouldn't last long and I needed him to come with me. I squeezed my muscles around his cock, leaned over, and attacked his neck. My fangs breached his skin, and his taste hit me like a dream. If possible, he almost tasted better than before. There was some kind of sweetness to it that tasted a lot like love.

He groaned, and I could feel his cock throb deep inside of me. Our whole bodies were in sync. His heart, cock, and my pussy throbbed in the same rhythm. I sucked up his blood as my orgasm washed over me and my pussy milked his cock. He thrust up a few more times and when he came inside of me, his teeth marked my neck.

The pleasure that was flowing through me together with his blood only became bigger when our mating bond snapped into place. I could feel it immediately. A strong sense of belonging washed over me as our bodies were locked together in our climax.

He was mine, and I was his. From this day forward, I would never be alone. I would always have Isaac as my Mate.

The End

Bonus Story: Going to a Naga Wedding

I hadn't known what to expect from a Naga wedding, but this was not it. Could you even call it a wedding when it resembled something more like an Orgy? I knew Naga's were free creatures, but I hadn't intended to see quite as much from the bride as I was seeing.

I looked at Ezra who was smiling. When he saw the look on my face, he visibly paled, his green scales getting a more ashen tone to them.

"Oh Gods, I should have warned you more right?"

I couldn't speak, too shocked. And I didn't think he would have even heard me over the sound of the moans and groans. He pulled me back outside. As soon as the fresh air hit me, I took a few staggering breaths. My cheeks felt flushed, my breathing was coming out in puffs, and I was... aroused. It was strange to say about your date's cousin, but seeing her get fucked was probably one of the hottest things I had seen in my life.

"I just need a second to wrap my head around it and then we can go back inside."

I was clutching the wedding gift, trying to get my thoughts in place. I had brought a salad bowl to an orgy. Well, not an orgy per se, a Naga wedding that started out with an orgy. Ezra had given me some details about how a Naga wedding worked, but I just hadn't realized he wasn't joking. Gods, I was an idiot, it was my first time dating a non-human and I was making an absolute fool of myself.

"I should have..."

I shook my head, grabbing his hand to stop his self-inflicting blame. The comforting hardness of his scales soothed me.

"No, no, I should have believed you. I just hadn't expected it to be so..."

The right words were lost to me. So hot? So arousing? So wrong, and yet so right? I didn't mean any disrespect to their culture but if we were to get engaged I didn't think I could do that. I shook my head, what was I even thinking about? We were only dating for a few months, we were not even close to that point in our relationship. Yet I felt like I could be myself around him, and my feelings for Ezra had grown so much in the short time we had known each other, I knew he was the one for me, but I wasn't sure he thought the same.

After taking a deep and steadying breath I looked him in the eyes. His slitted green eyes were filled with worry, and I felt bad for making him feel that way.

"We just need some rules. What do you expect from me? I'm all for monogamy so if that is not for you maybe we should..."

Ezra squeezed my hand and I saw a relieved look cross his face.

"No expectations. If you only want to go to the ceremony and dinner that is fine. If you want to go back in and join that is also fine. Or if you want to go in and watch it together with me that is also fine. I just want you to be comfortable, Avery."

I nodded my head and took another deep, calming breath. Okay, we could work through this like a healthy couple. Just communicate and look at each other limits.

"I think I want to watch, but I don't want anyone but you touching me." I caressed the back of his hand with my thumb and smiled at him. "Is that okay?"

He nodded and smiled. His face turned even more handsome when he showed of his fangs.

"Would it also be okay if I don't want you touching anyone?" I asked.

"Of course. I asked you to come with me so we could be together not so you could watch me fuck my cousin's best friend or something."

Ezra blushed and that put me so much at ease. He was still my Naga boyfriend. Cute, sometimes shy, and all mine. I laughed and gripped my gift tighter.

"Okay, let's do this."

When we entered the fuck fest was still going on. I could appreciate it more knowing that we wouldn't be actively participating with other people. The sounds that carried through the warm room were arousing. Breathy moans, growls, and the sounds of slapping flesh mingled together.

We checked in our clothes at the entrance and suddenly I was naked in a room filled with fucking creatures. I appeared to be the only human and a lot of hungry eyes turned to me.

I stepped closer to Ezra and gratefully accepted the yellow wristband. As soon as I put it on, the eyes drifted away. Everyone wore a color-coded wristband signaling if they belonged to the side of the bride or the groom and if they wanted to actively participate or not. Our yellow bands were a sign that we were here with the Bride and we weren't going to participate with anyone else but our partner.

It kinda felt like a weight being lifted off my shoulders and I could breathe and admire what was happening around me. Feeling Ezra beside me, put me at ease and simultaneously turned me on. His hardening cocks probed at my back as he pushed closer to me.

His breath tickled my ear as he whispered, "Let's find a quiet corner so we can watch and enjoy ourselves."

I nodded, breathlessly. Arousal rushed through me, and I knew that he was able to taste it in the air.

"You like watching people, don't you? Just like when we first met."

The memory of our first meeting in the library only turned me on more. I wanted him to fuck me just like that, filling both my holes, and making me forget about everything around me.

Ezra led me to a long bench that sat beside the outer wall. We had a good view of the room, and we weren't in the middle of the lovemaking. He sat on the bench and pulled me on his lap. I had to open my legs wide to accommodate his large tail. His cool scales, rubbed the insides of my thighs, creating shivers that pushed through my body.

I was on full display for all the creatures to see and I loved it. The room was filled with all kinds of monsters, Nagas, Minotaurs, Orcs, and Fairies, ... Everywhere I looked I could see different cocks and pussies, but all I really cared about were the two cocks behind me. Ezra pushed his hand between my legs and growled a low rumble of pleasure.

"You're already so wet for me."

I moaned in response, losing my words. I grabbed his neck behind me, needing something to hold on to, pushing my breasts upwards. My legs were trembling as he slid one of his scaly fingers inside of me. His other hand went to my breast, teasing my nipple until it was hard and throbbing. Pleasure filled me as he played my body like his own personal instrument. He switched to my neglected breast giving it the same type of attention, as he pushed two more fingers inside of me with his other hand.

"Where do you want my cocks today, Avery. In your mouth, your pussy, or one in your ass and one in your pussy?"

My pussy clenched around his fingers, as every scenario flashed before my eyes. Kneeling before him, with my ass to all the people fucking while sucking him off. Being double stuffed by him and screaming as I always did when both his cocks filled my pussy. Having both my holes filled and being a moaning mess in his arms. I wanted all of it. Turning my head to look into his beautiful green, serpent eyes, I realized I loved this Naga.

"What do you want?" I asked, stroking his cold cheek, loving the feel of his scales underneath my soft skin.

"I want to fill both your holes and feel you squeeze around my cocks as you moan my name."

My pussy squeezed his fingers and I made a soft sound full of need. "I want that too."

His hand left my pussy and went to his mouth. He licked his fingers, making the most obscene sounds possible. My eyes were focused on his mouth as both his tongues worked around his fingers. When they were slick with his saliva, he positioned his hand on my ass. He pushed one finger inside, slicking me with his spit. With practiced moves he added another and another finger, prepping my asshole to take his cock.

"Nice and tight," he growled.

Closing my eyes I focused on the feeling of his fingers, stretching me as arousal filled me. I knew his cock would be ten times better and I almost begged him for it, but he knew what I needed before I voiced my command.

He grabbed my hips and pulled me up, positioning his cocks at my entrances. I helped by directing them and in one fluent move he pushed both of them inside. My body trembled as pleasure filled my scenes. Both his cocks stretched me in the most delicious way. I was used to feeling him fill me like this, but it still made my breath hitch.

"You feel amazing around my cocks," he said with a strained voice.

Ezra gave me a moment to catch my breath before he grabbed my hips to move me on his lap. He lifted me up and dropped me back down, giving me amazing friction. Every thrust made the ridges on his cock fill me with pleasure and my breasts bounce. I moaned in unashamed pleasure, not caring how loud I was being.

"Everyone is looking at you," Ezra whispered in my ear. "Every single creature is jealous of me, but you're all mine."

I opened my eyes and he was right. Almost every face was locked on me. Arousal rushed through me as my pleasured sounds grew louder. I didn't know what I was moaning, but one constant was always on my lips, Ezra's name. Every time I uttered his name, he became a little wilder, a little more feral and our fucking became even better. The pleasure inside of me grew with each push and pull.

He was fucking me harder and I could feel his fingers leaving marks on my hips. I loved him marking me for everyone to see, claiming me as his.

"Mine," he hissed with every thrust, and I moaned in agreement.

My climax was fast approaching, but as always I needed just a little extra push to reach it. When my moans turned into pleasured cries, his tail slithered upwards between my legs. He circled my clit, sparking pleasure inside of me. Only he could give me pleasure like this, filling all of my holes and reaching all of my pleasure points at the same time.

"Come for me, Avery. Scream my name and let everyone know that I am yours."

His words were enough to push me over the edge. My body trembled, and my muscles clenched and squeezed his cocks as pleasure flowed through me. I screamed his name as waves of pleasure washed over me. I could feel his cocks throb inside of me, and after a few more thrusts he filled me with his cum. A hum of satisfaction slipped from my lips as I fell back against his chest. His arms surrounded me and I closed my eyes, basking in the aftershocks of my climax.

Every single moment I spent with Ezra just made me fall in love with him more and more.

The End

Authors Note

I love doing these little bonus story that follow up after each other. I have no idea where Ezra and Avery will go next, but I hope you enjoy their journey!

Thank you for buying this book and supporting an indie author! When I started writing monster erotica I never thought my imagination would keep flowing like this. I am so happy to be able to share my third creature loving volume and I wholeheartedly hope that you enjoyed the previous two and the many more to come!

About the author

Lilith Leana writes what she loves; Monster erotica.

Born and raised in Belgium, she devours ebooks as if it heals her. In her day job she loves to organize, plan and make schedules for other people, but when the night falls she can let loose with her fantasies which star all kinds of Monsters and Human couplings.

YOU CAN ALSO FIND ME on:
Author Home Page: https://lilithleanaauthor.start.page/
Instagram: https://www.instagram.com/lilithleana/
Or you can email me: lilith.leana666@gmail.com

DEAR READER

If you enjoyed this book, please consider leaving a review. Indie writers depend on reviews to keep writing and publishing.

Thank you so much ❤

Lilith

Also by the author

Series & Collections

Standalone Short Stories

---

1. https://books2read.com/u/47gLkj

2. https://books2read.com/u/47VMwA

3. https://books2read.com/u/3J6dxJ

4. https://books2read.com/u/3yVerv

5. https://books2read.com/u/mBvKok

6. https://books2read.com/u/bwrZN9

7. https://books2read.com/u/boy8vV

8. https://books2read.com/links/ubl/3kYPzN

9. https://books2read.com/u/md1P5w

10. https://books2read.com/u/b5jJAk

11. https://books2read.com/u/3LVqEX

Saved by the Yeti[13]
Mated to a Vampire[14]
Seducing the Orc[15]
Bedding the God of Dreams[16]
Saved by the Grim Reaper[17]
Chased by the Werewolf[18]
Trapped with the Yeti[19]
A Mate for the Vampire Queen[20]

Holiday Short Stories

Helping the Green Goblin Steal Christmas[21]
Catching Cupid[22]

Coming Soon

The House of Desire: Multiple part Series - Coming Soon - 2023

---

12. https://books2read.com/u/38PLpB

13. https://books2read.com/u/bQj7VP

14. https://books2read.com/u/m2d8Y6

15. https://books2read.com/u/bON1NE

16. https://books2read.com/u/4ARgJo

17. https://books2read.com/u/bxrZZo

18. https://books2read.com/u/bzKW7Z

19. https://books2read.com/u/bopvPZ

20. https://books2read.com/u/3R0Lgv

21. https://books2read.com/u/mZEGjR

22. https://books2read.com/u/ml8dvY

Brief summaries of other titles
by Lilith Leana

Taken by the Ghost[1]
When Alina meets a ghost in her shower, her first instinct is to scream, but her next...

Kristof has only one hour when the veil between the world of the living and the dead is thinnest. He is absolutely determined to make the most of his time in the land of the living.

Servicing the Minotaur[2]

Nova is late in returning her book. As she doesn't have the means to pay her fine, she comes to a pleasurable arrangement with the Minotaur librarian.

Tristan has always liked the shy little human. When she comes to him to ask for a payment plan for her fine, only dirty things cross his mind. He is sure they can work something out.

Saved by the Yeti[3]

Evelyn thinks her life is over when she gets trapped in the snow on her company ski trip. She gets saved by a massive white creature, and the moment she wakes up, the only thing she can think about is thanking her rescuer any way she can.

Jens the Yeti saved the cute little human female, trying to do the right thing. When she wakes up and rubs herself all over him, he can't resist his urge to breed her.

Mated to a Vampire[4]

---

1. https://books2read.com/u/3yVerv

2.	https://books2read.com/u/md1P5w

3.	https://books2read.com/u/bQj7VP

Luna Cassidy finds a Vampire in her territory who smells absolutely delectable. Her Wolf thinks he is her mate, but she doesn't want to give in to her urges before she knows why he crossed into her territory.

Elijah has to get to his Vampire Queen fast, but gets trapped in Wolf territory. When the sexy Luna tells him he is her mate, he scoffs and runs away, but something inside of him makes him turn back.

Don't miss out!

Visit the website below and you can sign up to receive emails whenever Lilith Leana publishes a new book. There's no charge and no obligation.

https://books2read.com/r/B-A-YTZU-AEOFC

BOOKS 2 READ

Connecting independent readers to independent writers.